2-13-17

Circle 'Round

5th Battalion D Co.

a Night Stalkers story

by

M. L. Buchman

Buchman Bookworks

Other works by M.L. Buchman

Get a free Starter Library at:
www.mlbuchman.com

Don't Miss a Thing!

Sign up for M. L. Buchman's newsletter
today
and receive:
Release News
Free Short Stories
a Free Starter Library

Do it today. Do it now.
http://www.mlbuchman.com/newsletter/

1

Chief Warrant 3 Lola Maloney stared at the tactical display of the DAP Hawk helicopter *Vengeance* projected on the inside of her helmet visor. Against the pitch dark of night outside the windshield and the soft glow of console instruments, the display revealed the rough terrain of the southern Ukraine and her broken flight formation.

The commander always knows what to do.

She tried it once more as a mantra, *The commander always knows what to do.*

Along with a thousand plus hours of officer training, none of it meant shit at the moment—she didn't have a goddamned clue what came next.

"Kara," she called to the drone operator tucked three hundred miles away on the USS *Peleliu* helicopter carrier, though her drone was circling somewhere six miles above *Vengeance*. "You're my eyes."

"Roger. All clear."

"Everybody else get down and land now."

At her radioed command, the three other birds descended to gather around the pair of already grounded heavy-lift Mil-17 Hind helicopters. One a shattered wreck and the other one was trying to salvage the bodies of the fallen.

Lola had "borrowed" both of them from the Iraqis for this mission. She hadn't been intending to return either one, but she hadn't planned on one being shot down either. Two bodies had been blown out through the fuselage, but there were still three bodies— she'd just think of them as bodies at the moment, not guys she'd handpicked and trained for this mission—trapped in there.

One thing Lola knew to the core of her being, she'd see the whole flight dead before she'd leave a body behind. Too much history had drilled that lesson into her head.

She had watched too much "News at 11" as captured pilots were tortured, raped, and even burned alive for "the cause"—whatever the cause of the week was. Had seen the old tapes of the bodies of dead pilots and Delta Force operators being dragged naked through the streets of Mogadishu.

That was not going to happen to her people.

If the ground team from the second Hind needed time to extract the casualties from the wreckage, she'd find it for them.

But on this flight, time was not their ally.

No one was.

The U.S. Army's 160th Special Operations Aviation Regiment drew the missions no one was supposed to know about, ever. And this one wasn't only supposed to be top secret, it could never be known that U.S. forces had been involved. The political ramifications would be horrendous. So they hadn't merely called SOAR, they'd called the edgiest company of all, the 5th Battalion D Company.

And the secret nature of the mission was why Lola had chosen the mix of craft that she had.

The Russian Mil-17 Hind transports—from the Iraqis but now sporting Ukrainian markings—and the three Kamov K-52 "Alligator" gunships—that the Georgian Air Force would be missing soon, repainted with Russian markings—had been the mask. The Alligators were supposed to pretend they were escorting the Hinds, or vice versa depending on which force they ran into…if they were unfortunate enough to run into anyone.

They were the working craft.

And her stealth-rigged, all black U.S. Army DAP Hawk, by far the most dangerous of them all, was the fist.

Once they were all parked on the bank alongside the river, she turned to Tim. Her husband—one of the unique features of the 5D that she'd never really understood was that married couples could fly together—had jumped to the front seat—from crew chief to copilot—earlier this year, and proved that he'd absolutely deserved the promotion.

"Keep the engines warm."

He nodded as she slid her helmet's visor up and disconnected the umbilical that tied her into the DAP Hawk's systems.

Her world, which had been a multi-layered tactical display across the inside of her visor, blinked out and left her blind in the total dark of a moonless night. Fumbling a bit, she pulled her night-vision gear out of its pocket on the inside of her door, snapped it into the helmet mount, and flicked it on. The world returned, in a hundred shades of bright green seen through the tunnel vision of infrared night-vision goggles.

Shedding her harness, she stepped down to the ground, which squelched under her feet. The first thing she checked was that her carbine rifle, with its stock folded neatly into place, still hung across her chest. The second thing was her helo's wheels. They'd sunk about a foot into the muck, but stopped there. They were parked in the bottomlands of the Kalmius River in the Eastern Ukraine.

The three Kamovs had landed, each just one rotor away, and appeared stable. Pilots measured small distances in rotor diameters, one rotor away meant they weren't going to engage each other's blades by accident. In combat, distances were often down to a half-rotor off some cliff face or power pole.

Rumor said that Major Emily Beale had once flown down to two feet off her rotor tips—on both sides at once—in combat. Lola still didn't know whether or not to believe that one, though with Emily...

The Kamov pilots opened their distinctive flat-paned canopy windows, but remained in their seats with the rotors at a bare idle. The fuel for this mission had been marginal at best, hovering over the delta during the entire recovery operation had not been an option, even if it turned them into sitting ducks.

She slogged to the downed Hind.

The sharp screech of battery-powered cutting tools hacking through the helo's aluminum and steel framework had her cringing, both the fingernails-on-a-chalkboard aspect and the way the sound seemed to echo into the night, as if rushing directly to the nearest enemy listening post.

A lone Ukrainian with an RPG had taken down the Hind as they'd been returning from their mission. One moment flying along in tight formation, and the next the Rocket-Propelled Grenade had turned the Hind helicopter into a tumbling ball of flame. She'd seen the track on her threat detector, clear as a laser across the inside of her visor.

She had dived onto that spot and, before they could reload, Big John had punched them down with two hundred rounds from the starboard side minigun. A matter of three seconds.

Three seconds that still echoed through the valley.

"Why can't the superpowers fight at home?" Trisha O'Malley strode up beside her.

"You're supposed to stay in your heli—" she shouldn't bother. Trisha never followed such orders, figuring they applied to the rest of the universe, but not her.

"But why?"

"How the hell am I supposed to know?"

The superpowers had been duking it out on other people's terrain since World War II had taught them battles at home were too expensive. America versus China in Korea, then Vietnam. Russia versus China in the Soviet War in Afghanistan.

And now the Ukraine.

But the Americans weren't here.

They couldn't be, neither officially nor even

by rumor, or it would be the start of America versus Russia, and nobody was ready for that.

Lola remembered the day the Majors had told her they were handing over command of the SOAR 5th Battalion D Company to her.

2

"You're shitting me!"

"We've told Command that you were the best qualified, and they agreed." Mark and Emily had taken her out for a lunchtime sail on the Chesapeake Bay that cloudless September day for "the talk."

She *hated* sailing.

Lunchtime or otherwise.

Though she was feeling a sudden antipathy for Major Mark Henderson that threatened to make that feeling trivial by comparison.

"W'all," Henderson pulled out that horrid fake Texas accent that he was dumb enough to think was cute and funny. "All y'all have ta do is—"

"Throw you overboard! Have you lost it, Henderson?"

He gave her one of *those* looks, raised eyebrows of mock surprise over his mirrored Ray Ban sunglasses.

"Sir!" she amended with a snarl.

His grin was electric, and if Emily hadn't been seated just to Mark's other side, Lola would have pushed him overboard. And then? She'd have figured out how to keep the sailboat going, leaving him to sink or swim in her wake.

"I'm the newest pilot on the team," her rage was turning into a knot in her stomach. "How the hell am I supposed to know what to do?"

Mark opened his mouth, and by the set of his smile Lola knew she really was going to dump his ass overboard this time—whether or not Emily was in the way.

Before she could lash out, Emily rested a hand on Mark's arm, "Remember that I told you there were times to shut up?" She didn't wait for his acknowledgement. "This is one of them."

And just like that, Major Mark "Viper"

Henderson was quelled. Damn, but Lola could use some tactical training on how to do that with her Tim.

3

"*Emily told me to* always protect my people," Lola looked down at Trisha. So close that she was a blinding green in the night vision—so bright it was almost as if she was an angel, which she so wasn't. "I suppose that means you as well."

"I don't need protecting. I need to not be an American soldier parked in the middle of an eastern Ukraine war zone with a lot of stolen Russian military equipment."

"Don't we all. You also need to be back in your Kamov."

Trisha opened her mouth.

"Now, O'Malley."

She snarled, but she went, which was about as pleasant as Trisha's mood ever was during a mission.

They pulled Jefferson out of the wreckage and lowered him into one of the body bags.

Don't think! she ordered herself. *Time for that later.*

They zipped up the bag and moved it to the intact Mil-17.

Lola edged in closer to assess the situation.

Ten tons of helicopter made one hell of a mess when it blew up and then crashed. The tail section lay twisted ninety degrees to the side, chunks of rotor blade scattered every which way.

The external fuel tanks had done their job and broken free on impact. Though they scented the air with the sharp bite of leaking kerosene, they'd landed far enough aside that it was safe to use cutting tools inside the cockpit and not worry about a stray spark blowing them to kingdom come.

The fuselage had shredded; the rear cabin exploded from the inside. The RPG had either entered through a window or penetrated the skin before going off. Sections of sheet metal were scattered far and wide.

The bulkhead between cabin and cockpit had blown forward, driving the pilot and copilot seats up against the forward consoles, pinning them in place.

They finished extracting the copilot. He too headed for a body bag.

One of the team recognized her and paused on their way back in to say, "Twenty minutes."

"Ten," was her automatic answer.

He nodded uncertainly, so she called after him, "Eight would be better."

She stepped out into the dark night. Checked that Trisha was back where she belonged. Good, at least one thing was going right.

Then she looked over at the open cargo bay of the surviving Hind. The three main honchos behind the rebel leadership of the breakaway, Russian-backed, Donetsk People's Republic were still safely under the watchful eyes of the Delta Force squad that had snatched them.

These men couldn't be safely assassinated, not by the CIA, Mossad, or anyone else she didn't want to know about. The powers-that-be feared that would make them martyrs to the cause. *But*, if they "apparently" defected, perhaps were occasionally photographed with high-ranking NATO officials, the blow to the rebel government would be significant. Or at least that's what the CIA analysts had spouted at her during the briefing.

They hadn't said a thing about what to do if some idiot rebel farmer with an RPG shot down a helicopter simply because he could—with no way to know if it was friend or foe—and killed five people and a much needed heli-asset.

She checked her watch. Thirty-four seconds had passed since she'd called eight minutes. She closed her eyes and tried to visualize everyone else flying out of here alive.

The image wasn't really coming together very well.

4

"If you protect your people," Emily had said that day as the sun shone off her blond hair, "as your number one priority, you will be amazed at what they will do for you."

One of the sails cracked almost as sharply as a gunshot as the forty-foot boat crested a wave and dropped off the other side. She flinched in alarm, but Henderson appeared to be in smooth control.

"I'm not you," Lola had pointed out. There wasn't a person in the 5D that wouldn't take a bullet for Emily Beale. There were only a half-dozen who could even tolerate Lola as far as she could tell...and she was married to one of them. That left five.

Emily, of course, did one of those answer-without-answering things and simply waited for Lola to put it together herself.

"Okay, not an idiot. Protect my people at all costs, and they'll learn to trust me."

Emily had nodded in that sage professorial way she had.

Lola had refused to ask the next question, though it was easy to see Emily waiting for it.

5

*"**If they trust me,**"* she muttered to herself, "then who do I—"

"Five minutes."

For a moment Lola thought it was the recovery crew with good news, but they were both still deep in the bowels of the shattered helicopter working frantically and she was halfway to the other Mil to check on the prisoners.

Then she connected that it was Kara's voice on the radio relay from the drone up at thirty-thousand feet.

"Crap! I need more time."

"Tell that to the Russians. You have three choppers and a fast mover out of Donetsk."

Lola really did not need to be fighting off a Russian jet with a bunch of stolen helicopters.

"Make that four minutes. Two more whirlybirds coming up out of Sevastapol in Crimea to the south."

"That was supposed to be our escape route. Shit!"

If Kara replied, Lola didn't bother listening. She sprinted back to the Mil-17, circling around the nose. The dead pilot's feet were sticking out where the lower front windshield had been. His head and upper body were out the main windshield. He must be trapped at the thighs by the way his body had been unnaturally folded.

A quick assessment of the metal still in the way and she knew that the estimate of twenty minutes had been an optimistic one.

Lola had traded in a career with Combat Search and Rescue to take a shot at SOAR. She'd made it. And you didn't do things like CSAR without knowing when to get drastic.

"Give me the saw!" she shouted at one of the ground crew.

6

"Anyone who's a decent commander can get someone to trust them, that's not the issue," Emily had handed her a crab salad sandwich, and Lola had managed not to throw it back in her face.

Mark was wisely keeping his mouth shut and paying attention to the boat.

But she wondered if he was purposely using his mirrored lenses to reflect the sun into her eyes so that he looked like a dazzle-eyed star lord, a terribly handsome one, but still. He was on the verge of having his sunglasses smeared with crab salad moving at high velocity when he appeared to think better of it and looked aside.

"The issue—" Emily very smoothly reached up and dropped an ice cube down the back of Mark's t-shirt.

His yelp made Lola feel much better.

"—is finding someone who can both command and think outside the box. Lola, you don't even see the box. That is your greatest strength."

7

Seventeen seconds later—when she was done with the saw—one of the ground crew had retched out his guts, but the last body bag was on the move. The results of the crash would have necessitated a closed-coffin funeral anyway, so whether he was in one part or—

Lola raced for her helicopter.

"Wind 'em up!" she called over the general frequency. She needn't have bothered, all of the helos were cranking their engines back up to speed as fast as they could once they saw her in motion.

Lola unharnessed her carbine as she slammed into her seat, reattached the data umbilical, and snapped on her harness. Just as she was about to pull off the night vision gear, she spotted the empty Mil-17 still sitting there, straight ahead. She should have dropped a couple of thermite grenades inside to make sure it was destroyed.

"Damn it!"

Tim, like the outstanding mind reader he was, must have noticed where her attention was. Two Hydra 70 rockets roared out of the right-hand pod of the DAP Hawk. Four-point-six pounds of high explosive blew into the Mil-17 at the speed of sound, along with a great deal of unspent propellant because the bird was so close. Then the spilled fuel lit off as well.

The fireball was impressive.

With her left hand she rammed the collective down to hold the DAP Hawk in place as the shock wave rolled over them. With the right, she shed her goggles and slid her visor back into place.

And on the tactical display saw that she was in hell.

She was the last one on the ground, so she yanked up for max lift, tipped her nose down as soon as she was aloft to gain speed and carved a climbing turn.

To the north, three helos, all Kamov KA-52s, and a fast mover jet.

To the south, two helos, both now identified as Mil-28 Havocs.

To the east, a pair of fast movers out of Berdyans'k.

Five of Russia's most advanced attack helicopters and three fighter jets. The way her luck was running…

Kara managed to ID the jets from her drone's feed: two Sukhoi Su-27s and an Su-30.

Would asking for a couple of nice thirty-year old MiG-21s fighter jets really be asking too much?

She had an overloaded Mil-17, three Kamov gunships, the DAP Hawk, and a drone.

They didn't stand a chance in hell.

This wasn't some stupid Hollywood tale where the good guys would eventually triumph. Or the noble few of the *Magnificent Seven,* who would survive to ride another day.

Even if this wasn't *A Nightmare on Elm*

Street, Freddy Krueger was going to plant his axe in the end zone.

She and the rest of her crew were about to get their asses kicked straight into their graves.

8

"The thing you don't appreciate, Lola," Mark was finally out of his snotty lecture mode, and was speaking as the commander… *former* commander of the most successful SOAR company in the regiment's history. A company he had built from the ground up.

This was a man she respected almost as much as his wife, if such things were possible. Which they weren't, but he did pretty well despite that handicap.

"You have a strategic mind. The 5D can't be commanded by a tactician. Tacticians always get thrashed when it gets really ugly. Keep your people at the forefront of your priorities. That's always the way through the problem."

Then he'd cracked that megawatt smile of his. "A'sides, worst that cain happ'n is y'all end up down a six-foot hole."

She'd already finished her sandwich, but the mug of ice tea had still been full enough to serve her purpose.

9

"You want out-of-the-box, Mark?" she said between gritted teeth and hauled up on the DAP Hawk's collective, pouring every trick she had into gaining max climb rate.

"What?" Tim asked from beside her.

She ignored him.

"You want stupid frickin' Hollywood? Fine, I'll give you stupid frickin' Hollywood!"

Tim, being a good copilot and a wise husband, kept his mouth shut.

The helicopters were a problem, but the jets were a disaster. They could move at Mach 2 and maneuver better than a BMW Mini.

Even the DAP Hawk could only go one-fifth the speed of a Sukhoi.

"Okay, folks," she got on the general frequency. "It is time to do what we do so well. Flight level is one hundred feet," though she kept climbing for all she was worth. "I want you to form up in a circle."

One thing Mark Henderson had always done a great job of was give the perfect amount of direction. A royal pain in the ass on the ground, but he was the master of the air. He never left a need for questions. But he also never said too much, thus trapping the flyers' actions into narrow boundaries.

"You are going to circle at one hundred feet above ground level as fast as you can go. Topography goes down, you go down. It goes up, you climb. If they come at you from above, Kara and I will take them." *Or do our damnedest.* "They come at you from the side, don't break formation to chase them. Your main firepower is facing forward. You shoot dead ahead as you circle. When they're out of your sights, they'll be in the sights of the helo circling right behind you. Trisha."

"Here, boss."

"You're my chaos demon," which was definitely what the woman was. "I want everyone on her tail. She circles more to the east, you shift with her. She circles to the south, you follow. Trisha keep that circle moving back and forth so they can't get a fix on you."

"Roger that."

Already Lola could see them setting up a four-helo spinning top; one Hind and three Kamovs. When they fired their weapons they'd be like a spinning buzz saw of rockets and flying lead.

Her tactical display said less than thirty seconds until bad news arrived. And the Russians had set up the pincer well, they'd be arriving from three directions at once; no chance of escape.

"Tighten it up. Keep close together. I want your gap under one rotor between helos."

Even as she said it, they tightened up. They were now moving fast and began rolling back and forth over the river valley and the steep banks. Every ten to twelve seconds they made a full spin, shifting back and forth along the river like the circle itself was alive.

Nobody but a SOAR team could fly like that.

10

One of the Sukhoi fast movers came in fast and low, thinking the four helos spinning over the landscape like a psychotic, whirling dervish were an easy target.

Trisha fed it a Russian Vympel R-73 air-to-air missile from her KA-52's spread of weaponry before it knew what was happening.

Dennis killed the first enemy Kamov attack helicopter, and Lola didn't have time to spare to see what happened to the other three attack helos that came in low, but there was a hell of a lot of fire being exchanged in her peripheral vision—enough to light up the wide river valley in brilliant stroboscopic splashes that wreaked havoc on her helmet's night-vision display.

Her real concern was up high and she kept climbing for the DAP Hawk's service ceiling and to hell with the fuel reserve as she clawed for altitude.

Lola was trying to set up the sleight-of-hand, knowing the most dangerous attack would be coming down from high above, if only she could get up into position in time. She had dealt the game for the bad guys to see, four cards face up along the river valley and spinning in their circle.

But she'd kept two cards hidden up her sleeve.

The apparently easy target was the circling helos…to anyone at their altitude. Viewed from above they were an easy and, more importantly, an obvious target.

Two of the jets and one of the massive Mil-28 Havoc gunships came in high to do just that.

The stealth DAP Hawk had been built for only one reason, to shoot better than anything else on the planet. Only SOAR had the Direct

Action Penetrators and as far as Lola knew, the *Vengeance* was the only surviving stealth model—after the loss of one in bin Laden's compound, and the other that had almost killed the now-retired Majors.

Of the two jets who'd thought to attack from above, the first one had come in very high.

Kara's drone carried four Hellfire missiles and she launched them all.

Two of them tore up the Sukhoi Su-23.

That left a jet and a helo attacking from above, and Lola had a single drone with no more ammunition and her own DAP Hawk.

The formidable Su-30 jet rolled into a dive, aimed straight down at the spinning circle of helicopters from above. That was the reason Lola had Trisha shifting them side-to-side, to make them a harder target in case Lola's plan didn't work. Not that it would buy them more than a few seconds of life, but it might be all she needed.

The second jet flew right past the DAP Hawk never realizing it was there. Tim sent a phalanx of six Hydra 70s into the belly of the beast as it plunged downward.

Three connected and blew off its wing, sending the jet into a death spiral.

The Mil-28 Havoc pilot who had come in high was good, very good. The Havoc dodged hard when he saw the Su-30 get shredded.

But Lola's bird cast almost no radar image and regrettably for him, he guessed wrong about her location. The Russian helo ate a barrage from Tim's Vulcan 20mm cannon.

But before he died, the Russian pilot managed to launch an Igla-1V missile straight down at the buzz saw of helos still alight with their own battle.

Lola put herself between the missile and her people. She couldn't risk flares or chaff, because if the missile decided to ignore the distractors, it would hit her team circling below.

She couldn't force the nose of her helo to bear on the missile in time. So she rolled the DAP Hawk onto its side, exposing herself broadside to the missile.

Lying on her back in the crew-chief's seat behind Lola, with her minigun pointed straight up and firing six thousand rounds a minute, Connie killed the missile only a few rotors before it would have slammed into the *Vengeance.*

The heat blast was intense. The shockwave of the exploding missile flipped them out of the sky like they were a swatted fly.

Engines flamed out.

She and Tim fought to restart them.

Hydraulic systems failed as shrapnel sliced through crucial lines.

Backups kicked in. Stabilized. Held.

It took her fifteen thousand feet of tumbling freefall to recover. No time for fear. She leveled out only moments before she would have augered in—right through the center of her team's spinning circle.

Lola achieved a stable hover less than two rotors above Trisha's dervish and scanned the tactical display.

The other helos still whirled at top speed, rolling back and forth over the landscape. And, thank god—there were still four of them.

Scattered far and wide across the river valley there were fires and, Lola's night vision revealed, piles of overheated wreckage. No one was moving. No parachutes had deployed. There would be no witnesses to the bloodbath that had occurred on the bottomlands of the Kalmius River this night. No one to report who had actually been here.

"Status?" she managed—against a very dry throat—to ask those circling below her.

Two of her crewmembers were hit but alive. One of their prisoners had been killed when a 30mm round passed through the cabin of the Hind right where his head had been, but the others were alive.

Kara reported the airspace clear from her view high above.

Lola lined them up, gave a big sigh, and they turned once more for the coast, moving fast and low.

She would raise her next glass of beer in a toast westward, where the Majors had retired to fight forest fires in Oregon and raise their daughter in safety. That was in her and Tim's future, but not yet.

Lola now knew that Mark and Emily were absolutely right. The way through any problem? Protect your people, no matter what the personal cost. And against all odds it had worked; they'd survived.

"How did you think of that buzz saw thing

anyway?" Trisha's radio call broke in on Lola's train of thought.

She blew out a long, slow breath and made sure she kept the adrenaline shakes out of her voice as she did her best to imitate Major Mark Henderson's notoriously bad fake Texas accent.

"W'all…"

Everyone recognized it right away and laughed, some more shakily than others.

"I jes had y'all pull them wagons inta a circle, don'cha know."

About the Author

M. L. Buchman has over 50 novels and 40 short stories in print. Military romantic suspense titles from his Night Stalker, Firehawks, and Delta Force series have been named Booklist "Top 10 Romance of the Year": 2012, 2015, & 2016. His Delta Force series opener, Target Engaged, was a 2016 RITA nominee. In addition to romance, he also writes thrillers, fantasy, and science fiction.

In among his career as a corporate project manager he has: rebuilt and single-handed a fifty-foot sailboat, both flown and jumped out of airplanes, and designed and built two houses. Somewhere along the way he also bicycled solo around the world.

He is now making his living as a full-time writer on the Oregon Coast with his beloved wife and is constantly amazed at what you can do with a degree in Geophysics. You may keep

up with his writing and receive a free starter
e-library by subscribing to his newsletter at:
www.mlbuchman.com.

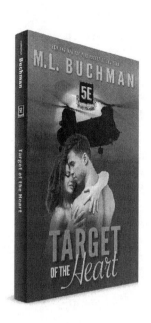

Target of the Heart (excerpt)
-a Night Stalkers novel-

Major Pete Napier hovered his MH-47G Chinook helicopter ten kilometers outside of Lhasa, Tibet and a mere two inches off the tundra. A mixed action team of Delta Force and The Activity—the slipperiest intel group on the planet—flung themselves aboard.

The additional load sent an infinitesimal

shift in the cyclic control in his right hand. The hydraulics to close the rear loading ramp hummed through the entire frame of the massive helicopter. By the time his crew chief could reach forward to slap an "all secure" signal against his shoulder, they were already ten feet up and fifty out. That was enough altitude. He kept the nose down as he clawed for speed in the thin air at eleven thousand feet.

"Totally worth it," one of the D-boys announced as soon as he was on the Chinook's internal intercom.

He'd have to remember to tell that to the two Black Hawks flying guard for him…when they were in a friendly country and could risk a radio transmission. This deep inside China—or rather Chinese-held territory as the CIA's mission-briefing spook had insisted on calling it—radios attracted attention and were only used to avoid imminent death and destruction.

"Great, now I just need to get us out of this alive."

"Do that, Pete. We'd appreciate it."

He wished to hell he had a stealth bird

like the one that had gone into bin Laden's compound. But the one that had crashed during that raid had been blown up. Where there was one, there were always two, but the second had gone back into hiding as thoroughly as if it had never existed. He hadn't heard a word about it since.

The Tibetan terrain was amazing, even if all he could see of it was the monochromatic green of night vision. And blackness. The largest city in Tibet lay a mere ten kilometers away and they were flying over barren wilderness. He could crash out here and no one would know for decades unless some yak herder stumbled upon them. Or were yaks in Mongolia? He was a corn-fed, white boy from Colorado, what did he know about Tibet? Most of the countries he'd flown into on black ops missions he'd only seen at night anyway.

While moving very, very fast.

Like now.

The inside of his visor was painted with overlapping readouts. A pre-defined terrain map, the best that modern satellite imaging could build made the first layer. This wasn't some sort of a crappy, on-line, look-at-a-picture-of-your-house video display. Someone had a pile of dung outside their goat pen? He could see it, tell you how high it was, and probably say if they were pygmy goats or full-size LaManchas by the size of their shit-pellets if he zoomed in.

On top of that were projected the forward-looking infrared camera images. The FLIR imaging gave him a real-time overlay, in case someone had put an addition onto their goat shed since the last satellite pass, or parked their tractor across his intended flight path.

His nervous system was paying autonomic attention to that combined landscape. He also compensated for the thin air at altitude as he instinctively chose when to start his climb over said goat shed or his swerve around it.

It was the third layer, the tactical display that had most of his attention. At least he and the two Black Hawks flying escort on him were finally on the move.

To insert this deep into Tibet, without passing over Bhutan or Nepal, they'd had to add wingtanks on the Black Hawks' hardpoints where he'd much rather have a couple banks of Hellfire missiles. Still, they had 20mm chain guns and the crew chiefs had miniguns which was some comfort.

While the action team was busy infiltrating the capital city and gathering intelligence on the particularly brutal Chinese assistant administrator, he and his crews had been squatting out in the wilderness under a camouflage net designed to make his helo look like just another god-forsaken Himalayan lump of granite.

Command had determined that it was better for the helos to wait on site through the day than risk flying out and back in. He and his crew had stood shifts on guard duty, but none of them had slept. They'd been flying together too long to have any new jokes, so they'd played a lot of cribbage. He'd long ago ruled no gambling on a mission, after a fistfight had broken out about a bluff hand that cost a Marine three hundred and forty-seven dollars. Marines hated losing to Army no matter how many times it happened. They'd had to sit on him for a long time before he calmed down.

Tonight's mission was part of an on-going campaign to discredit the Chinese "presence" in Tibet on the international stage—as if occupying the country the last sixty years didn't count toward ruling, whether invited or not. As usual, there was a crucial vote coming up at the U.N.—that, as usual, the Chinese could be guaranteed to ignore. However, the ever-hopeful CIA was in a hurry to make sure that any damaging information that they could validate was disseminated as thoroughly as possible prior to the vote.

Not his concern.

His concern was, were they going to pass over some Chinese sentry post at their top speed of a hundred and ninety-six miles an hour? The sentries would then call down a couple Shenyang J-16 jet fighters that could hustle along at Mach 2 to fry his sorry ass. He knew there was a pair of them parked at Lhasa along with some older gear that would be just as effective against his three helos.

"Don't suppose you could get a move on, Pete?"

"Eat shit, Nicolai!" He was a good man to have as a copilot. Pete knew he was holding on too tight, and Nicolai knew that a joke was the right way to ease the moment.

He, Nicolai, and the four pilots in the two

Black Hawks had a long way to go tonight and he'd never make it if he stayed so tight on the controls that he could barely maneuver. Pete eased off and felt his fingers tingle with the rush of returning blood. They dove down into gorges and followed them as long as they dared. They hugged cliff walls at every opportunity to decrease their radar profile. And they climbed.

That was the true danger—they would be up near the helos' limits when they crossed over the backbone of the Himalayas in their rush for India. The air was so rarefied that they burned fuel at a prodigious rate. Their reserve didn't allow for any extended battles while crossing the border…not for any battle at all really.

* * *

It was pitch dark outside her helicopter when Captain Danielle Delacroix stamped on the left rudder pedal while giving the big Chinook right-directed control on the cyclic. It tipped her most of the way onto her side, but let her continue in a straight line. A Chinook's rotors were sixty feet across—front to back they overlapped to make the spread a hundred feet long. By cross-controlling her bird to tip it, she managed to execute a straight line between two mock pylons only thirty feet apart. They were made of thin cloth so they wouldn't down the helo if you sliced one—she was the only trainee to not have cut one yet.

At her current angle of attack, she took up less than a half-rotor of width, just twenty-four feet. That left her nearly three feet to either side, sufficient as she was moving at under a hundred knots.

The training instructor sitting beside her in the copilot's seat didn't react as she swooped through the training course at Fort Campbell, Kentucky. Only child of a single mother, she was used to providing her own feedback loops, so she didn't expect anything else. Those who expected outside validation rarely survived the SOAR induction testing, never mind the two years of training that followed.

As a loner kid, Danielle had learned that self-motivated congratulations and fun were much easier to come by than external ones. She'd spent innumerable hours deep in her mind as a pre-teen superheroine. At twenty-nine she was well on her way to becoming a real life one, though Helo-girl had never been a character she'd thought of in her youth.

External validation or not, after two years of training with the U.S. Army's 160th Special Operations Aviation Regiment she was ready for some action. At least *she* was convinced that she was. But the trainers of Fort Campbell, Kentucky had not signed off on anyone in her trainee class yet. Nor had they given any hint of when they might.

She ducked ten tons of racing Chinook under a bridge and bounced into a near vertical climb to clear the power line on the far side. Like a ride on the toboggan at Terrassee Dufferin during Le Carnaval de Québec, only with five thousand horsepower at her fingertips. Using her Army signing bonus—the first money in her life that was truly hers—to attend *Le Carnaval* had been her one trip back to her birthplace since her mother took them to America when she was ten.

To even apply to SOAR required five years of prior military rotorcraft experience. She had applied after seven years because of a chance encounter—or rather what she'd thought was a chance encounter at the time.

Captain Justin Roberts had been a top Chinook pilot, the one who had convinced her to switch from her beloved Black Hawk and try out the massive twin-rotor craft. One flight and she'd been a goner, begging her commander until he gave in and let her cross over to the new platform. Justin had made the jump from the 10th Mountain Division to the 160th SOAR not long after that.

Then one night she'd been having pizza in Watertown, New York a couple miles off the 10th's base at Fort Drum.

"Danielle?" Justin had greeted her with the surprise of finding a good friend in an wholly unexpected place. Danielle had liked Justin—even if he was a too-tall, too-handsome cowboy and completely knew it. But "good friend" was unusual for Danielle, with anyone, and Justin came close.

"Captain Roberts," as a dry greeting over the top edge of her Suzanne Brockmann novel didn't faze him in the slightest.

"Mind if I join ya?"

A question he then answered for himself by sliding into the opposite seat and taking a slice of her pizza. She been thinking of taking the leftovers back to base, but that was now an idle thought.

"Are you enjoying life in SOAR?" she did her best to appear a normal, social human, a skill she'd learned by rote. *Greeting someone you knew after a time apart? Ask a question about them.* "They treating you well?"

"Whoo-ee, you have no idea, Danielle," his voice was smooth as...well, always...so she wouldn't think about it also sounding like a pickup line. He was beautiful, but didn't interest her; the outgoing ones never did.

"Tell me." *Men love to talk about themselves, so let them.*

And he did. But she'd soon forgotten about her novel, and would have forgotten the pizza if he hadn't reminded her to eat.

His stories shifted from intriguing to fascinating. There was a world out there that she'd been only peripherally aware of. The Night Stalkers of the 160th SOAR weren't simply better helicopter pilots, they were the most highly-trained and best-equipped ones on the planet. Their missions were pure razor's edge and black-op dark.

He'd left her with a hundred questions and

enough interest to fill out an application to the 160th. Being a decent guy, Justin even paid for the pizza after eating half.

The speed at which she was rushed into testing told her that her meeting with Justin hadn't been by chance and that she owed him more than half a pizza next time they met. She'd asked after him a couple of times since she'd made it past the qualification exams— and the examiners' brutal interviews that had left her questioning her sanity, never mind her ability.

"Justin Roberts is presently deployed, ma'am," was the only response she'd ever gotten.

Now that she was through training— almost, had to be soon, didn't it?—Danielle realized that was probably less of an evasion and more likely to do with the brutal op tempo the Night Stalkers maintained. The SOAR 1st Battalion had just won the coveted Lt. General Ellis D. Parker awards for Outstanding Combat Aviation Battalion *and* Aviation Battalion of the Year. They'd been on deployment every single day of the last year, actually of the last decade-plus since 9/11.

The very first Special Forces boots on the ground in Afghanistan were delivered that October by the Night Stalkers and nothing had slacked off since. Justin might be in the 5th battalion D company, but they were just as heavily assigned as the 1st.

Part of their training had included tours in Afghanistan. But unlike their prior deployments, these were brief, intense, and then they'd be back in the States pushing to integrate their new skills.

SOAR needed her training to end and so did she.

Danielle was ready for the job, in her own, inestimable opinion. But she wasn't going to get there until the trainers signed off that she'd reached fully mission-qualified proficiency.

The Fort Campbell training course was never set up the same from one flight to the next, but it always had a time limit. The time would be short and they didn't tell you what it was. So she drove the Chinook for all it was worth like Regina Jaquess waterskiing her way to U.S. Ski Team Female Athlete of the Year.

The Night Stalkers were definitely a damned secretive lot, and after two years of training, she understood why. With seven years flying for the 10th, she'd thought she was good.

She'd been repeatedly lauded as one of the top pilots at Fort Drum.

The Night Stalkers had offered an education in what it really meant to fly. In the two years of training, she'd flown more hours than in the seven years prior, despite two deployments to Iraq. And spent more time in the classroom than her life-to-date accumulated flight hours.

But she was ready now. It was *très viscérale,* right down in her bones she could feel it. The Chinook was as much a part of her nervous system as breathing.

Too bad they didn't build men the way they built the big Chinooks—especially the MH-47G which were built specifically to SOAR's requirements. The aircraft were steady, trustworthy, and the most immensely powerful helicopters deployed in the U.S. Army— what more could a girl ask for? But finding a superhero man to go with her superhero helicopter was just a fantasy for a lonely teenage girl.

She dove down into a canyon and slid to

a hover mere inches over the reservoir inside the thirty-second window laid out on the flight plan.

Danielle resisted a sigh. She was ready for something to happen and to happen soon.

* * *

Pete's Chinook and his two escort Black Hawks crossed into the mountainous province of Sikkim, India ten feet over the glaciers and still moving fast. It was an hour before dawn, they'd made it out of China while it was still dark.

"Twenty minutes of fuel remaining," Nicolai said it like a personal challenge when they hit the border.

"Thanks, I never would have noticed."

It had been a nail-biting tradeoff: the more fuel he burned, the more easily he climbed due to the lighter load. The more he climbed, the faster he burned what little fuel remained.

Safe in Indian airspace he climbed hard as Nicolai counted down the minutes remaining, burning fuel even faster than he had been while crossing the mountains of southern Tibet. They caught up with the U.S. Air Force

HC-130P Combat King refueling tanker with only ten minutes of fuel left.

"Ram that bitch," Nicolai called out.

Pete extended the refueling probe which reached only a few feet beyond the forward edge of the rotor blade and drove at the basket trailing behind the tanker on its long hose.

He nailed it on the first try despite the fluky winds. Striking the valve in the basket with over four hundred pounds of pressure, a clamp snapped over the refueling probe and Jet A fuel shot into his tanks.

His helo had the least fuel due to having the most men aboard, so he was first in line. His Number Two picked up the second refueling basket trailing off the other wing of the Combat King. Thirty seconds and three hundred gallons later and he was breathing much more easily.

"Ah," Nicolai sighed. "It is better than the sex," his thick Russian accent only ever surfaced in this moment or in a bar while picking up women.

"Hey, Nicolai," Nicky the Greek called over the intercom from his crew chief position behind Pete. "Do you make love in Russian?"

A question Pete had always been careful to avoid.

"For you, I make special exception." That got a laugh over the system.

Which explained why Pete always kept his mouth shut at this moment.

"The ladies, Nicolai? What about the ladies?" Alfie the portside gunner asked.

"Ah," he sighed happily as he signaled that the other choppers had finished their refueling and formed up to either side, "the ladies love the Russian. They don't need to know I grew up in Maryland and I learn my great-great-grandfather's native tongue at the University called Virginia."

He sounded so pleased that Pete wished he'd done the same rather than study Japanese and Mandarin.

Another two hours of—thank god—straight-and-level flight at altitude through the breaking dawn and they landed on the aircraft carrier awaiting them in the Bay of Bengal. India had agreed to turn a blind eye as long as the Americans never actually touched their soil.

Once standing on the deck—and the worst

of the kinks had been worked out—he pulled his team together: six pilots and seven crew chiefs.

"Honor to serve!" He saluted them sharply.

"Hell yeah!" They shouted in response and saluted in turn. It was their version of spiking the football in the end zone.

A petty officer in a bright green vest appeared at his elbow, "Follow me please, sir." He pointed toward the Navy-gray command structure that towered above the carrier's deck. The Commodore of the entire carrier group was waiting for him just outside the entrance. Not a good idea to keep a One-Star waiting, so he waved at the team.

"See you in the mess for dinner," he shouted to the crew over the noise of an F-18 Hornet fighter jet trapping on the #2 wire. After two days of surviving on MREs while squatting on the Tibetan tundra, he was ready for a steak, a burger, a mountain of pasta, whatever. Or maybe all three.

The green escorted him across the hazards of the busy flight deck.

Pete had kept his helmet on to buffer the noise, but even at that he winced as another

Hornet fired up and was flung aloft by the catapult.

"Orders, Major Napier," the Commodore handed him a folded sheet the moment he arrived. "Hate to lose you."

The Commodore saluted, which Pete automatically returned before looking down at the sheet of paper in his hands. The man was gone before the import of Pete's orders slammed in.

A different green-clad deckhand showed up with Pete's duffle bag and began guiding him toward a loading C-2 Greyhound twin-prop airplane. It was parked number two for the launch catapult, close behind the raised jet-blast deflector.

His crew, being led across in the opposite direction to return to the berthing decks below, looked at him aghast.

"Stateside," was all he managed to gasp out as they passed.

A stream of foul cursing followed him from behind. Their crew was tight. Why the hell was Command breaking it up?

And what in the name of fuck-all had he done to deserve this?

He glanced at the orders again as he stumbled up the Greyhound's rear ramp and crash landed into a seat.

Training rookies?

It was worse than a demotion.

This was punishment.

Available at fine retailers everywhere.

Other works by M.L. Buchman

41510010R00045

Made in the USA
Middletown, DE
15 March 2017